USBORNE HOTSHOTS

SWIMMING

USBORNE HOTSHOTS

SWIMMING

Edited by Lisa Miles
Designed by Nigel Reece

Illustrated by Roger Fereday,
Shelagh McNicholas and Tessa Land

Series editor: Judy Tatchell
Series designer: Ruth Russell

Based on material by Emma Fischel, Susan Meredith,
Carol Hicks and Jackie Stephens

CONTENTS

Into the water

If you are still learning to swim, here are some ideas on how to start. Go to the pool with an adult who can help you. Don't go to the pool alone if you can't swim.

Getting started

Go to a pool where the water is warm and comes up between your waist and shoulders. Don't stay in the pool for too long – 45 minutes is enough. You will learn better in short sessions, rather than long ones. Don't swim if you are ill.

Armbands can be useful if they make you feel at ease in the water. Only wear them for part of a session and as you progress, let some air out each time. Goggles can be helpful if the water stings your eyes, though try to do without.

Learning in shallow water

To gain confidence, walk on your hands along the pool bottom in very shallow water. Kick your legs as you go. As you become braver, try taking your hands off the bottom. The water should be no deeper than 30-45cm (12-18in) for this.

Floats

In deeper water, you can try using a float to help you swim.

This is a shaped piece of plastic which will not sink in water. It is designed so that you can hold onto it easily, so it helps you stay afloat.

Getting in

To get into deeper water without a ladder, sit on the edge of the pool. Rest both hands to one side of you.

Then turn around and slide into the water. Once you're in, bob up and down so that the water laps around you.

Safety

- Never run along the poolside or push people.
- Don't startle swimmers by jumping in too close to them, splashing or grabbing them.
- Never try to duck other people.*

On your front

To get used to being on your front in the water, hold onto the edge, then kick your legs up and down. Then try holding a float out in front and kicking your legs. Or you could hold a float under each arm and kick.

On your back

To get used to being on your back, hold a float under each arm or one on your tummy and kick. Try to lie back, relaxing your neck and pushing your tummy up.

5

*For more tips on safety, see pages 29-31.

Starting to swim

Once you are used to swimming with a float or with someone helping you, try swimming by yourself. Here's how to start.

Breathing

First, try to get used to putting your face underwater. This makes it easier to swim properly and you will be less put off by splashes from other swimmers. Breathe in when your face is out of the water and breathe out when your face is in the water.

Pushing and gliding

Stand in the water a short distance from the edge, facing the poolside.
Push off with your feet from the pool bottom and glide to the edge with your arms and legs outstretched. As you gain confidence, gradually increase your distance from the edge and put your face in the water.

To push off from the edge, ask a partner to stand facing you a short distance away. Hold onto the edge, put your feet on the wall, then push off and glide to your partner. Try this on your front and back.

Using your arms

Most people start swimming using a "dog paddle" type of stroke. Keeping your hands in the water and your fingers together, pull each hand toward you. Try to feel that you are "fastening on" to the water just before you pull.

Sculling

Learn how the water reacts to your hand movements by sculling. Stand with your shoulders and hands underwater. Press your palms back smoothly with your thumbs by your thighs. Then turn your hands and pull them forward again, with your thumbs outermost.

Begin to swim

Ask an adult to support you under your armpits while you pull with your arms and kick your legs up and down. As you get confident, ask your helper to support you with just two fingers of each hand or to take their hands away completely.

Don't worry too much about your swimming style at this stage. Once you can swim at least 10m (30ft) on your own, you can think about starting to learn the strokes described later in this book.

Putting your feet back down

From your front, lift your head, tuck your knees up and press down with your hands.

From your back, lift your head and tuck your knees up. Push your palms up in front of you.

The crawl

The crawl, sometimes known as the front crawl, is the fastest of all the strokes. It is the natural stroke to progress to from the dog paddle, so it is probably the best stroke to try first.

Body position

This picture shows the ideal body position to aim for during the crawl. It helps you to swim smoothly.

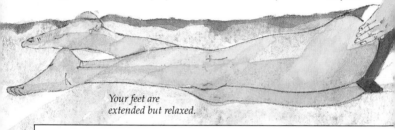

Keep your hips just under the surface.

Your feet are extended but relaxed.

The stroke

1. Slide your right arm into the water with your elbow high. Your hand slices the water in front of you.

2. Begin to bend your right elbow. As you do this, your left thumb should be brushing your thigh.

3. Lift your left arm out of the water by bending your elbow. Pull your right arm down and back. Keep your elbow bent.

The leg kick

Hold on to the edge and try to perfect your leg kick.

Kick up and down in a whipping action. Kick from your hip, not your knee. Try to keep going without pausing.

Relax your ankles and turn your feet in if you can. Don't let your feet go any higher than just breaking the surface.

Your body is streamlined and stretched.

Rest your shoulders on the surface.

The water surface should cut between your eyebrows and hairline.

Point your nose ahead.

Most of the forward movement is created by your arms.

4. While your left arm comes down, bring your right arm down and back, bending your elbow as you pull.

5. Slide your left arm into the water as you push your right arm back in the direction of your hip.

6. Lift your right arm out of the water, elbow first, and start to press your left arm down through the water.

Breathing

Take your breath quickly.

In the crawl, you can either breathe to the left or the right. As your arm leaves the water, your shoulder lifts up and helps you turn your head to breathe.

As your head turns out of the water, breathe in quickly. Return your face to the water and breathe out gradually through your nose and mouth.

The breaststroke

The breaststroke is a less tiring stroke than the crawl. For this reason, it is used for lifesaving.

Body position

Your body should be as flat and streamlined as possible. You have to lift your head up to breathe.

Turn the soles of your feet up at the start of the leg action.

Don't let your feet break the surface when you kick.

The stroke

1. Glide with your legs straight, your arms extended and pressed against your ears, and your face in the water.

2. Sweep your hands out, back and down but keep them in front of your shoulders. Lift your head and breathe in.

3. As you sweep your hands down, keep your thumbs pointing down. Keep your elbows bent and legs straight.

Arm actions

A common mistake in the breaststroke is to sweep your arms out sideways and flat. The correct positions are shown on the right. Try them out standing in shallow water.

1. Your elbows bend but stay high while the hands pull back and down, palms facing your feet.

2. When your hands are beneath your elbows, they move in together and up.

3. Your palms are now facing each other. Turn them down to begin the glide (stage 1 above).

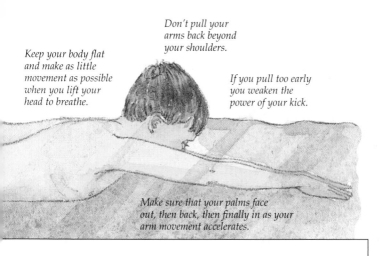

Keep your body flat and make as little movement as possible when you lift your head to breathe.

Don't pull your arms back beyond your shoulders.

If you pull too early you weaken the power of your kick.

Make sure that your palms face out, then back, then finally in as your arm movement accelerates.

4. Sweep your hands in, palms facing each other, to below your chin. Bend your knees so your heels rise up.

5. As you push your hands to the front, turn your feet out and sweep them out and back in a whip-like action.

6. If it suits you, hold this stretched, streamlined position for a glide before starting again with the arm action.

Foot position

Most of the power in the breaststroke comes from your legs. To make your kick stronger, try getting your feet angled in the correct positions, as shown on the right.

1. Draw your feet up, with your knees pointing down and your soles facing up.

2. Keep your feet turned out and your ankles bent as you push your heels back and out.

3. As your legs straighten, turn your soles up to streamline your legs as you bring them together.

11

The backstroke

Strokes that are swum on the back are called backstrokes. The most popular backstroke, sometimes known as the back crawl, is used by competitive swimmers. When you swim on your back, check before you start that there is no one behind you.

Body position

This picture shows an ideal body position to aim for. The body is streamlined and stretched flat.

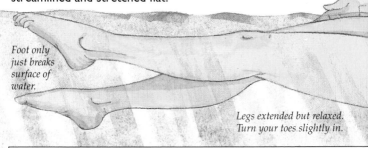

Foot only just breaks surface of water.

Legs extended but relaxed. Turn your toes slightly in.

The stroke

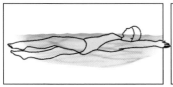 

1. Slide your left hand into the water with your arm straight. Place your right arm along your body, thumb up.

2. Press your left arm down and out in a circular path as you lift your right arm out of the water.

Breathing

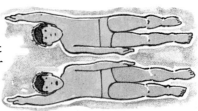

Breathing in the backstroke is fairly relaxed. Breathe out as one arm enters the water and in as the other enters. Open your mouth wide to get plenty of oxygen.

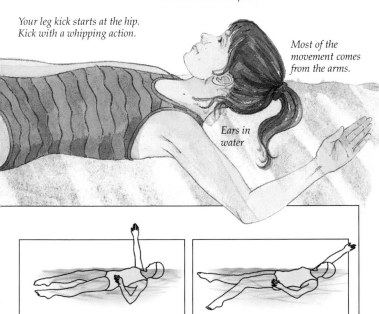

Rest your head as if it were on a pillow, with your chin tucked slightly into your neck. Look up and back down the pool.

Your leg kick starts at the hip. Kick with a whipping action.

Most of the movement comes from the arms.

Ears in water

3. Sweep your left arm down, with your palm facing your feet. Then push your hand to your thigh until your elbow is straight.

4. Straighten your left arm as you sweep it in the direction of your thigh, ending with a strong push.

Timing the stroke

There are usually six leg kicks to each arm cycle. That is, three leg kicks to each arm pull. The opposite leg kicks down at the start of each arm pull to balance the body.

Kick strongly to balance the arm action.

13

Floating

Floating is an energy-conserving survival skill. It is also useful for gaining confidence in the water. Some people find floating easier than others, depending on their size and weight. The key to successful floating is to relax completely. Start in shallow water, so that you can put your feet down quickly if necessary.

On your back

Lie on your back in the water with your arms by your sides. You may need to make gentle sculling movements, until you get your balance and feel buoyant (held up in the water). It might be easier with your arms and legs in a star shape.

Mushroom float

Lie on your front, take a deep breath in and then tuck up into a ball, clasping your arms around your legs.

On your front

Take a breath and then lie with your face in the water, either with your arms and legs outstretched or in a star shape. Lift your head to breathe when you need to.

Floating vertically

When you have mastered the other floats, experiment with this one. Try it in fairly deep water from the start.

Get into a vertical position as shown on the right. Then simply put your head back so that your mouth and nose are just above the surface of the water.

When trying this float, you may need to scull gently to stay in place.

Floating practice

If you find floating difficult, try holding two floats, either at arms' length or under your arms, depending on which position you are floating in.

Treading water

Treading water is another way of staying in one place and using as little energy as possible. It is useful to be able to do this in case you get into any difficulties.

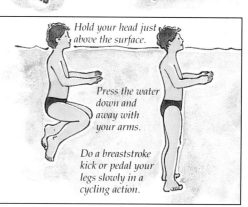

Hold your head just above the surface.

Press the water down and away with your arms.

Do a breaststroke kick or pedal your legs slowly in a cycling action.

Starting to dive

To do these dives, the water must be at least 1.8m (6ft) deep. For dives beyond those shown on pages 16-19, you must have lessons*. Never dive without an adult present.

Surface diving

To do this, first take a deep breath and stretch out on your front. Make a quick breaststroke arm pull, bend at the hips and plunge your head and shoulders down.

As your legs start to come out of the water, straighten at the hips, so your legs are in the air. Push your arms forward until they are outstretched and in line with your body.

The weight of your legs will drive your body down into the water. Make another breaststroke pull if you want to go deeper, but don't kick with your legs until they are underwater. To get into a horizontal position to swim underwater, turn your fingers up.

*Ask about diving lessons at your local pool.

Underwater

When learning to dive, you need to feel confident swimming and turning under the surface with your eyes open. Try these exercises for practice.

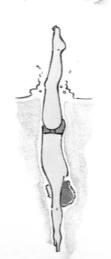

Push off from the wall and glide through a partner's legs.

Try walking on your hands on the bottom of the pool.

There are three ways of swimming underwater.

- Breaststroke arm and leg action.
- Breaststroke arm action with crawl leg action.
- Dog paddle arm action with crawl leg action.

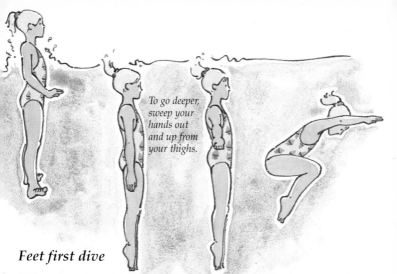

To go deeper, sweep your hands out and up from your thighs.

Feet first dive

Take a deep breath and give a vigorous kick to raise your body high out of the water.

With legs together, toes pointed and arms by your sides, let your body drop below the surface.

When deep enough, draw your knees up to your chest, lean forward and start swimming.

Surfacing again

To surface, do a strong breaststroke leg kick and press down with the palms of your hands. If necessary, put your arms above your head and pull them down strongly to your sides first.

Jumping in

Increase your confidence even more by jumping in from the side of the pool, forward and backward. Or, you could enter the water in some different ways, shown below.

Slide in like a seal.

Do a forward roll into the pool. Don't lift your head.

Roll in sideways like a log.

17

More dives

In the dives here, aim for a smooth entry into the water, followed by a shallow glide. Don't try to go too deep. Remember, don't try anything more advanced unless you are taught by a trained coach.

Sitting dive

1. Sit on the side, with your feet on the wall. Point your arms at the pool, with your head tucked down.

2. Roll forward. Press firmly away from the side with your feet. Glide into the water.

The kneeling dive

1. Kneel on one knee, gripping the pool edge with your other foot. Point your fingers forward and tuck your head down.

2. Overbalance and push off with your left foot. Stretch your body and bring your legs together.

The lunge

1. Stand with your front leg bent, but your back leg straighter. Grip the edge with your toes.

2. Overbalance and push off with your front leg. Lift your back leg, then bring both legs together.

18

Diving safety

- Only dive in a pool. You can easily misjudge the depth of a river or the sea.

- Always check that the water is deep enough. It should be at least 1.8m (6ft) deep for the dives shown here.

- Never play in a diving area and always check that there are no swimmers in the way when you dive.

- Take it slowly. Only when you have mastered simple dives should you move on to more advanced ones.

- A belly flop happens if you hold your head too high when you take off. Your body smacks down flat on the water. To avoid this, tuck your head into your chest as you dive.

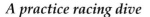

A practice racing dive

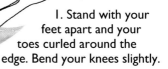

This dive forms the basis for a racing dive, which you might use to start a swimming race. The full dive is described on page 20.

1. Stand with your feet apart and your toes curled around the edge. Bend your knees slightly.

2. Swing your arms so that your body leans forward and your knees bend. Push off hard from the poolside with a strong drive from your legs.

3. As your feet leave the side, try to straighten your body. Keep your legs streamlined.

4. Enter the water. When your feet are underwater too, lift your head and point your fingers up to surface.

Climbing out

Get used to climbing out of deep water without a ladder. Put your hands on the side.

Bob in the water and haul yourself up until your arms are straight and supporting you.

Then pull one knee out of the water and onto the side. Pull the other knee out and stand up.

Swimming races

Swimming races are often won by narrow margins. Here are some tips for a strong start and finish, which can both save you vital seconds.

The racing dive

This is the most popular forward start.

Listen for the starting signal. Don't look around.

1. Stand on the starting block, with knees bent, feet apart and toes curled around it. Hold it with your hands, between or outside your feet. Keep your hips forward. At the signal, pull hard on the block.

2. As you overbalance, drop your knees and straighten your arms. Raise your head and look down the pool. When your knees are nearly level with your feet, push off hard from the block.

3. Lower your head to keep streamlined. Bend slightly at the highest point of the dive and enter the water.

Body position

On entering the water, try to keep as streamlined as possible, with your hands close together and your fingers pointed. Keep your head between your arms and your ankles stretched.

The finish

Finishing relies on split-second judgment. You may have to decide quickly whether to start a new stroke or lengthen the current one.

- As you approach the end of the pool, kick hard, then reach out for the wall.

- To save time, touch the wall with your fingertips, not your palm.

- Both hands must touch together in the breaststroke and the butterfly. In the crawl and the backstroke, you touch with just one hand.

The backstroke start

For a backstroke race, you start in the water. Here's how to make a racing start.

1. Hold the edge and, if it suits you, put one foot slightly higher than the other. On "take your marks", pull yourself up into a crouched position.

2. Push hard on the edge to start. Push with your feet so your bottom rises clear of the water. As you leave the wall, throw your head up and back and your arms up and out.

3. As your hands enter the water, arch your back. Glide with your arms stretched out. Start kicking and go smoothly into the stroke as you surface.

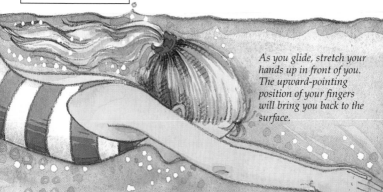

As you glide, stretch your hands up in front of you. The upward-pointing position of your fingers will bring you back to the surface.

Diving competitions

If you are interested in entering diving competitions, you need to work with a qualified coach. Some of the techniques can be hard to learn, but here is some information to give you an idea of what's involved.

This photo shows a diver performing a backward dive. She will enter the water head first, facing away from the board.

Types of dives

- Forward dive. Start facing forward on the board.
- Backward dive. Start facing back.
- Armstand dive. Start from a handstand on the board.
- Reverse dive. Take off forward, but twist in the air to face away from the board.
- Inward dive. Start facing back, go into a pike, then enter water vertically facing away from the side.
- Twist dive. You twist your body around in the air. All dives can have twists in them.

Takeoff, flight and entry

Each dive can be divided into three — takeoff, flight and entry. The time the diver spends in the air is called the flight. A diver can be straight, tucked or piked in flight.

You can enter the water head or feet first, but the body must be as straight and vertical as possible.

Tucked. Rolled up into a ball, bent hips and knees.

Straight. Fully stretched with no bending.

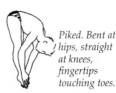

Piked. Bent at hips, straight at knees, fingertips touching toes.

22

Competition dives

There are six different groups of competitive dives, one on the highboard and five on the springboard. Competitors do a mixture of set dives and voluntary dives chosen from recognized groups.

Judges look for diving technique, ability, personal style and interpretation. Dives are marked out of ten, with decimals to one place. Judges show their marks either on an electronic scoreboard or by holding cards up.

Tips for top divers

- Top divers need strong ankles and legs to provide power for a good takeoff. They train regularly with weights to build strength.

- Most divers use trampolines for diving practice. During practice at the poolside, they often use mini-trampolines to give themselves extra lift on takeoff.

This diver is in the middle of flight, just about to enter the water.

Water polo

Water polo is fast and exciting. Many pools have teams and train beginners. You must be able to swim well to play.

How to play

There are two teams of up to eleven players each. Only seven of each team play at any one time. You score by putting the ball in the other team's goal. You mustn't touch the bottom of the pool.

There are four five-minute periods of play. If there is a tie at the end, the teams have a five-minute break and then play extra time.

Goal

Goal line

2m (6½ ft) line

4m (13ft) line

Half-distance line

Players must score from outside the 2m (6½ ft) line.

Goalkeepers can stand on the bottom inside their own 4m (13ft) line.

Free throws and corners

A free throw is given to the opposing side if the ball goes out of the pool or hits the side and bounces back in.

A corner is given when a defender sends the ball over his or her own goal line. The nearest attacking player then takes the corner from the 2m (6½ft) line.

Ball control tips

It is harder to control a ball in water than on land.

• Keep your arm almost straight behind your shoulder to throw.

• To pick up the ball, push it down. As it bobs up, put your hand under it and scoop it up.

• Swing your arm back to cushion the ball as you catch it.

Synchronized swimming

Synchronized swimming is doing dance movements to music while swimming. To try it, you need to be able to scull well (see page 7). You also need a good sense of rhythm as well as flexibility and stamina.*

How to do it

Synchronized swimmers combine various strokes and arm and leg movements, set to music, to create patterns and shapes in the water. The movements are all arranged beforehand.

Solo swimmers move in time, or synchronize, with the music. Group swimmers synchronize with both the music and each other.

Small speakers under the water allow the swimmers to hear the music while they perform their movements.

This position is called an inverted vertical. It requires enormous strength and stamina.

Judging

Judges award points out of ten. Teams get an extra half point for every swimmer above four, as synchronization is harder. Touching the pool bottom loses you a point.

This is called the back tuck position. It can form the start of a back tuck somersault.

*Ask at your local pool for synchronized swimming clubs.

Swimming practice

To improve your swimming and your confidence in the water, you could try some of these exercises. Make sure that you aren't going to get in the way of other swimmers first.

Somersaulting

Somersaulting is a good way to improve your underwater confidence. Push off from the pool edge with your feet, then somersault underwater, keeping your eyes open as you do so.

Explosive breathing

Stop if you feel any strain.

Good swimmers use "explosive breathing" to force air in and out of their lungs. Breathe in as quickly as you can, then put your head underwater and breathe out as hard as you can. Repeat several times to get used to the feeling.

Gliding underwater

To improve your glide, push off strongly from the wall of the pool. Concentrate on keeping your body streamlined as you glide and return to the surface as smoothly as possible.

Get a friend to measure how far you glide as you improve.

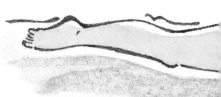

26

Breaststroke kick check

Lie on
your back,
holding a
float under
each arm to
keep you
stable. Try your
breaststroke kick,
watching to see
that your legs are doing
the right movements and
working together.

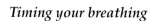

Timing your breathing

To learn how to breathe
without upsetting your
stroke rhythm, hold a
float and start kicking. Place
your face in the water, then lift it up to breathe
out and in. Kick as evenly as you can, as you do so.

Backstroke arm action

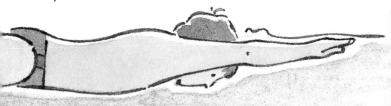

As you become better at the backstroke, try this exercise.
Hold a float to your chest with one arm and concentrate
on using your free arm well. Swap the float around and
then try it with the other arm.

Games

Here are some games for you to play in the water with your friends. Be extra careful not to get in the way of others and also make sure that an adult is supervising your group.

Statues

You have to stand still when "it" touches your arm or leg. You can only be "unfrozen" by another player swimming through your legs. When everyone has been caught, the one who has been a "statue" the longest becomes "it".

Still pond

Everyone floats as still as possible while one person watches. The last one to move is the winner.

Duck underwater

For underwater confidence, hold hands in a circle. One player squeezes the next person's hand, who then ducks underwater. She comes up and squeezes the next one's hand. This continues around the circle.

Pool safety

Swimming is great fun, but remember that water can be dangerous.

Remember not to go swimming right after a meal. Allow about an hour to digest your food.

Dos and don'ts

Here are some dos and don'ts for swimming in a pool. Always try to be thoughtful about other swimmers.

- Do check that there are no other swimmers around if you are jumping or diving in.

- Do try to look where you are going, so that you don't collide with anyone.

- Do be careful if you are using equipment such as flippers or snorkels. Flippers can hurt people and snorkels can make you lose your sense of direction.

- Don't run around the pool edge. You could slip over or fall in.

- Don't dive in shallow water.

- Don't duck people. It can shock them and destroy their confidence.

More safety tips

Never swim anywhere alone, even in a pool. If you have any doubts about safety, then don't swim. Here are some safety tips for swimming in rivers and seas.

Note where the lifebelts or other emergency aids are kept.

Don't swim near piers or breakwaters. Currents and waves around them can be very strong.

Open water is usually colder than a pool, so don't stay in for a long time.

Swim parallel to the shore. If you swim out to sea, you may be too tired to swim back.

Obey notices and flags which show you where or where not to swim.

Stay clear of boats. You may not be seen from the boat and they can't change direction quickly.

If you are in difficulty

If you find yourself in difficulty, here is some basic advice. If you want to learn more about lifesaving, you could join a course*.

First, try to stay calm. Decide on your safest form of action. You may decide just to stay afloat until help comes. Try to move as little as possible by treading water (see page 15). You can attract attention to yourself by waving one arm.

If you decide to swim to safety, lifesaving backstroke is good to use if you are feeling tired. To do this, swim on your back and use a slow breaststroke kick. Scull with your hands.

*Ask at your local pool for lifesaving courses.

Someone else in difficulty

If you see someone else in difficulty, try to keep calm. Shout for help or get someone else to go and get help. Don't get in the water yourself if you can rescue the person without doing so. Speak to the swimmer calmly and give clear instructions.

Near the edge

If the swimmer is near the edge, lie down flat and grab his or her wrist. Hold onto something secure. If someone else is there, they should hold your legs.

Out of reach

If the swimmer is too far out to reach, look for something to extend your reach, such as a stick, towels or clothes knotted together. Lie down as you haul the person in.

If he or she is too far out to reach, throw something that will float, such as a beach ball or plank. Don't aim directly at the swimmer, but make sure it lands within reach.

Hauling someone out

If the person can't get out of the water on his own, hold onto his wrists and bend your knees. Lift him up and down two or three times, and then lift him over the edge, letting him rest on your leg first, before you lower him to the ground. Protect his head as you do this. Lift his legs over the edge.

Index

Acknowledgements

The publishers would like to thank the following for permission to reproduce their photographs in this book: Cover, Professional Sport Ltd; p.22, Empics; p.23, Empics; p.24 Allsport UK; p.25 top, Richard J. Sowersby; p.25 bottom, Empics.

Additional illustrations by Joe McEwan.